Banjo and Alvin started hiking up a lonely mountain road toward the deserted spar mine, a place so dangerous every kid in town had been warned to stay away from it.

But Banjo knew it was where they might find the old hermit Jake Horse, the famous person they had chosen for their school project.

People whispered about Jake but nobody was brave enough to talk to him.

Before the day was out the two boys were to learn a lot about danger and bravery, and friendship, too.

# ·BANJO·

# Books by ROBERT NEWTON PECK

*A Day No Pigs Would Die*    *Patooie*
*Path of Hunters*    *Soup for President*
*Millie's Boy*    *Eagle Fur*
*Soup*    *Trig Sees Red*
*Fawn*    *Basket Case*
*Wild Cat*    *Hub*
*Bee Tree* (poems)    *Mr. Little*
*Soup and Me*    *Clunie*
*Hamilton*    *Soup's Drum*
*Hang for Treason*    *Trig Goes Ape*
*Rabbits and Redcoats*    *Soup on Wheels*
*King of Kazoo* (a musical)    *Justice Lion*
*Trig*    *Kirk's Law*
*Last Sunday*    *Trig or Treat*
*The King's Iron*    *Banjo*
*Secrets of Successful Fiction*

ROBERT NEWTON PECK

# ·BANJO·

Illustrated by ANDREW GLASS

Alfred A. Knopf
NEW YORK

THIS IS A BORZOI BOOK PUBLISHED BY ALFRED A. KNOPF, INC.

Text Copyright © 1981, 1982 by Robert Newton Peck
Illustrations Copyright © 1982 by Andrew Glass
Manufactured in the United States of America
4 6 8 0 9 7 5

Library of Congress Cataloging in Publication Data
Peck, Robert Newton. Banjo.
Summary: While doing research for a school essay
about a reclusive old mountain man,
two boys fall into an abandoned mine shaft
from which only the old man can rescue them.
[1. Mountain life—Fiction.  2. School stories]
I. Glass, Andrew, ill.  II. Title.
PZ7.P339Ban 1982  [Fic]  82–15347
ISBN 0–394–85394–6  AACR2  ISBN 0–394–95394–0 (lib. bdg.)

*I dedicate this book to a great guy
who will always be my pal . . .
and I'll always be his . . .
Fred Rogers* (TV's Mister Rogers)

# ·BANJO·

# · One ·

"Go, team, go!"

I couldn't believe what I saw. There was our chubby teacher, Miss Crowder, holding an old beat-up football and yelling, pretending she was a cheerleader.

"Ziss, boom bah!" Standing in front of our class, Miss Crowder actually jumped up in the air an inch or two. As she landed, the boards of the school floor groaned some. The schoolhouse was one room, and Miss Crowder darn near filled it.

A picture of George Washington dropped silently off the wall.

But did that stop Miss Crowder? Heck, no. Once she got started and really engined up about homework, nothing ever stopped our teacher, short of a foot-thick wall. She appeared to be out of breath; yet she went on hollering, louder than if she'd smelled smoke.

"Yes, we're going to write a *theme*. So—pick your team!"

Even though Miss Crowder dropped the football, by mistake, she was still smiling at us. A kid just had to like her. Leastwise, I did. Yet I wasn't too happy about what was coming up.

"A theme?" Doris Crump asked.

"Right!" Miss Crowder doubled a fist and punched the air, even though all the kids in the room, all twenty-three of us, were groaning. If there was one word I hated, it was *theme*. Whenever I had to compose one, all I could ever think up to write down was my name— Alvin Dickinson.

"It'll be fun," said Miss Crowder, who was bending over, trying to retrieve her bouncing football. She fumbled again, and mumbled something about some general we could study, Robert E. Lee.

"How long?" asked Fletcher Larkin.

"Long doesn't count," Miss Crowder told him. "What matters is how *well* we write it. And how much *fun* we make it."

We all moaned.

Failing to capture the football that was still wobbling across the floor like a wounded duck, Miss Crowder finally kicked it into the corner. I don't know why I did it. I just clapped. So did Banjo, the kid who sat in front of me.

"Now then," Miss Crowder said as she slowly regained her breathing, "what we're all going to do is pick a famous character to write about. But first, pick a teammate. You'll do the research together, but *each* of you writes a theme. Got it? Two kids on every team."

Just about every freckle on my body, and I must have sported at least a thousand, was aching to pick Agnes Halloran. But she was only the prettiest gal in the town of Freemont, along with maybe a few other planets beside Earth. I figured she wouldn't pick me. So I just sat there.

"Nobody'll pick Banjo."

Hearing those three words whispered behind me, I wanted to turn around in my seat and tell Ida Trowbridge that nobody'd pick *her* either. But as I thought it I knew she was right. Who'd pick a crazy kid like Banjo Byler, who never heard of taking a bath and hardly ever took the banjo off his back? We all ducked him as much as possible.

I heard Agnes Halloran pick Fletcher Larkin.

Miss Crowder looked my way. "Alvin . . ."

"Yes'm."

"Have you picked anyone yet?"

That was when I stood up beside my seat, shot my ferocious tiger look at Ida and spoke out in a loud voice. Just about louder than I'd ever said anything in my entire life. Even though I was still a soprano.

"Yes'm. I pick Ferguson Byler."

"Fine," said Miss Crowder.

Once, a few weeks back, I took notice of the sky, and how the sun poked through with a real determined yellow on the tail of a thundershower. That was how Banjo's face was now looking back at me. Sort of like a dirty old empty pie tin that suddenly had a fresh pie in it, made out of sugar and lemon and grin.

"Thanks," he said. Not very loud and only with his lips. "Thanks a lot, Alvin."

Some of the mean kids were snickering because we all knew that Banjo Byler never got to sit with anyone or got picked for a game. Not even out back in the school yard. I was his first team.

Looking off to the side as I sat down, I was sort of praying that Agnes Halloran would look at me as if I was a hero or a cowboy or something. No dice. She was too busy looking at Fletcher Larkin who probable took pretty pills.

"Well," said Miss Crowder, "it would appear that each of us has a teammate."

As she said it, I felt like every eye in the room was

staring at me, and it sure made my head itch. I scratched it. To make matters worse, I also began to itch in another place, too; but I don't guess I was fixing to scratch too much. Leastwise, not in school. Maybe it felt great to be one of the Byler kids.

They scratched anything everywhere anytime.

We all knew why. All you had to do was be in the same room with a Byler and your nose would tell you, sudden quick, that you weren't alone. And the way Banjo was scratching, right now, it sure was easy to see that *he* wasn't alone. There was some wildlife in his hair.

Still, I wasn't sorry I'd picked him.

Neither was Miss Crowder. Because just as I was leaving school that Friday, ready to spurt for home and chores, Miss Crowder shot out an arm to rein me back. She gave me five words and a wink.

"Alvin, you're growing real tall."

# · Two ·

*Whack!*

My hammer hit my thumb and it made me blurt out a real sorry word.

My swearing bounced around our cellar and finally died. I stood in silence at Dad's workbench, feeling my left thumb become a drum. It was pounding harder than the hammer. And there stood the nail, straighter than a tin soldier, with almost a smile on its little round head.

"Now," yelled my mother.

"Aw, can't I stay down here for ten more minutes? It's Friday night."

"Very well. *Ten minutes*, and not *one* second longer, or I'll tell your father."

"Yes'm."

At the top of the stairs the door closed; then, a second later, I heard her shoes walk back to the kitchen sink. Water hummed through our boiler tank.

Thumb or no, I'd have to work fast. With a little luck I might be able to stretch the ten more minutes into fifteen. Our kitchen clock above the sink was busted, and nobody'd fixed it.

The board I was sawing was hard wood.

I should have used soft. The crosscut saw snagged a tooth with every pull or push. What I was aiming to saw was half the roof of my birdhouse, which was intended to be a Mother's Day present. It had to be finished soon as time was already wading into May.

"Oh, well," I said with a sigh, "if I don't do her finished in time, I'll just switch it over to a Christmas present." The idea made me smile because I'd been laboring on this pesky birdhouse for at least five hundred years.

No chance of working on it tomorrow. I was meeting Banjo out at his place so that we could start to think

about a character for our themes. He'd said he had a
real brainstormer.

The saw blade bent.

I took a minute out to squirt some 3-in-One oil on its
rusty metal. A few drops wandered onto the bib of my
shirt. Then I screwed the little red cap over the spout
of the oil can and gave the board one more lick.

As I worked, I thought about Banjo. Maybe I was a
nut. Maybe you can't help anybody who's beyond help.
Perhaps all that Banjo Byler was ever fated to do was
grin, pick his banjo, and scratch. He'd never been
known to tackle much homework. And nobody in our
little school knew what grade he was in. Not even Miss
Crowder.

"Alvin Dickinson!"

"Be right up, Mom. Honest. Just as soon as I can get
the edge of my roof cut."

She sighed. "With you it's always something. It's
never *now*. By the time that birdhouse is done I'll be in
my grave. And so will the birds."

"No, you won't. Come on downcellar and take a look
at how I'm coming along. Maybe you'll spot what's
wrong."

My mother, wearing her faded green apron, clumped
down the cellar stairs, a red and white dish towel
thrown over her left shoulder.

"Don't think you're fooling me," she said. "You're only trying to borrow more time. Alice Trowbridge says that Ida goes to bed every night on the stroke of eight. And always says her prayers."

"Well," I said, "yippee for Ida Trowbridge."

"Don't be sassy, Alvin."

I bent the saw again, thinking about sweet little Ida whispering, "Nobody'll pick Banjo." Maybe old Banjo didn't even know the first word of a prayer. Well, it didn't matter a rat's rump to me. His grin today looked holier than every word that Ida Trowbridge ever faked on her knees.

"I'm not sassy. I just was feeling sorry that you and Dad couldn't be blessed with a swell kid like Ida to raise up."

Mom touched my arm. "Don't be silly. I have no intention of raising anyone but you and Marybell and your father."

"Good." I smiled at my mother's joke. "Seeing I'm the only boy you got, plus Bell who goes to bed earlier than chickens."

"That's no way to talk about your little sister."

"Bell's a pest."

"Do you have any arithmetic to do?"

"Some. But please, not on Friday night. Okay?"

Mother sighed again. "I know. Not on Saturday night

either. You'll leave it untouched until Sunday night and then remember it at bedtime."

I forced a smile at her. "Always do."

Mom looked at the wristwatch she pulled from her apron pocket. "It's near to ten o'clock. You said at supper that you're planning on getting up early."

"I am. But first I thought I might just take a stab at painting part of the birdhouse roof."

Mom closed her eyes. "But first. *But first.* Alvin Dickinson, you are going to but-first us all to death." Tossing a loop of her dish towel over my head, Mom hauled me up the cellar stairs the way you'd yank a mule on a halter. "Upstairs," she said. "Wash your hands and face. And don't wake Marybell. One child still up at this hour is about all I can abide." Her mouth popped open. "Just look at the front of your school shirt."

"It's only oil."

My mother closed her eyes, inhaled a very slow breath, then walked over to me and kissed me on the forehead. It made me smile up at her.

"The birdhouse I'm making is for Mother's Day. But it's really supposed to be a surprise."

Mom nodded. "I know. You've only told me about it a hundred times."

"I hope you'll love it a whole lot," I said.

"I'll love it even more than the birds."

# · Three ·

I brushed my teeth a full five seconds.

No use, I was figuring, in wearing out my new yellow toothbrush. Actually, it wasn't too new. It only looked it.

"Alvin, are you in bed?" my mother's whisper floated up the stairs.

Making a looping swan dive onto my quilt, I yelled, "Yes! I'm almost asleep." I shouldn't have shouted. That was one heck of a big mistake as it woke up Marybell.

"I want a drink of water," she said in a sleepy little voice.

This last bit of news pulled my father away from the radio. He didn't sound too joyful. In fact, I heard a swear word. Only one, but it was a real zinger.

"Alfred Dickinson," I heard Mom say to him in that same tone she used when she'd seen oil on my shirt. To me, Mom's life always sounded as though it was chock full of surprises.

"Bed!" My father yelled up the stairs.

"I'm getting Marybell a drink."

"Then be quick about it," Dad barked, "and I don't want to hear one more peep from either one of you unless you want me to charge upstairs."

"You bet. Good night."

I handed a pink Mickey Mouse cup half full of water to Marybell, then stood there, waiting for her to either drink it or spill it in her bed. She usual did both. I watched her drink one swallow and dribble three.

Her face frowned at the cup. "The water's warm. You didn't let it run to get cool."

"You're not supposed to complain about it, Bell. Just say thanks."

"Thanks." She handed me the cup.

"You're welcome. Now go to sleep. Do you know what time it is?"

"No." She rubbed her eyes. "You know I can't tell time yet. I'm too little."

"Good night."

"Alvin, tell me a story."

"No!" I whispered a holler at her. "It's a way too late. So don't be a brat."

"If you don't, I'll scream. And then when Mom runs up here, I'll tell that you made me spill the water."

As I stood in Marybell's room, holding a pink Mickey Mouse cup, I wondered what the jail sentence was for really whopping the tar out of a little sister. No jury, I was figuring, would have the heart to convict me. Not if they'd met Bell.

"Okay," I told her. "Pipe down."

"Then you'll tell me a story?"

"A short one."

"No, I want a long one. Tell me about that old guy who lives up on the mountain and never comes to town."

"You mean Jake Horse?"

Eyes widening, she nodded at me.

"Well," I said, sitting on the edge of the wet bed, "here goes. But you have to lie down and close your eyes to listen."

"Why?"

"Because that's the way you do it."

Sitting up straight, Marybell planted both fists to her hips. "You're kidding, Alvin. I hear lots of stories with both my eyes and ears open."

"Do you want the story or don't you?"

"I want it." She closed her eyes. "Right now."

"Then listen. Once upon a time, there used to be a spar mine out near the end of Hanson Road."

"Up the mountain."

"That's right. Now be quiet or I'll shorten the story. The mine's still there, but all the miners went away, soon after the spar vein ran dry. Only one old miner stayed. And now—he's a hermit."

"Old Jake Horse."

I nodded. "Some people claim he's part Indian, and some say no. Leastwise, he's up there, living all alone with only a mule for company. In a shack. He sleeps all day. But he comes out at night as soon as it gets real dark."

"What's he do?"

"Folks say he sits himself down on a juniper rock, on a bed of green moss, picks his banjo, and sings his old mountain songs up at the moon."

"What does he eat?"

Leaning forward, I whispered into Marybell's ear. "Banjo Byler told me that old Jake Horse eats only one thing."

"What's that?"

"He eats little girls."

Bell's eyes popped open. "Honest?"

I nodded. "Whenever old Jake Horse gets real hungry, he climbs aboard his mule and rides downroad, right here to Freemont, and peeks into bedroom windows."

Turning her head on the pillow, Marybell glanced over at the drawn curtains. To see her do it made me gloat inside. She sure was easy to buffalo.

"Does he use a ladder?"

"No need. Jake Horse just stands up real tall, on the back of his mule, and looks into any window he wants."

"Is he tall?"

"Well, old Jake isn't very tall."

"Good." Marybell let out a breath.

"But his mule is. Banjo says that Jake Horse's mule is near a foot taller than a ladder. About ten- or twelve-foot big."

"How'd he get so tall?"

"Eating cats. But old Jake won't eat cats or catfish. Whenever he spies a little girl like you in bed, he just jumps right through the window, opens up his great big mouth, and—"

Marybell screamed.

"Alvin Dickinson," I heard my mother holler from downstairs, "are you in your sister's room pestering her again?"

"She wanted to hear a story, Mom. Honest."

"What kind of awful story were you telling her?" My mother's voice was, I guessed, about two or three steps up the stairs.

"One about a mule."

# · Four ·

"Eat up," said my mother.

Squinting so I wouldn't have to look at the bowl, I spooned my eleventh spoon of breakfast oatmeal into my mouth and gagged it down. Oatmeal and I were deadly enemies. It was probably invented to poison rats.

"How much more do I have to eat?"

Mom said, "Every single bite, Alvin Dickinson, unless you want to stay cooped in your room all day."

It was Saturday. My favorite day of the week, as it gave me a breather between five days of Miss Crowder and a Sunday morning with Reverend Jarmin. Saturday, to me, was a hunk of Heaven, paid in advance.

I sure didn't want to be grounded and have to waste a Saturday as sunny as this one indoors. Not with what Banjo and I had planned. Mom's voice was warning me that she wasn't in too tolerable a mood, considering how I scared the jeepers out of Marybell last night with my Jake Horse story. To be honest about it, the idea of old Jake's prowling around our house in the dark didn't let *me* sleep too restful. It had kind of given me the midnight shivers.

Marybell was still upstairs asleep. That would help matters a mite. At least she wasn't down here in the kitchen to repeat the whole spooky tale to Mom.

I gulped down my oatmeal.

Yet before I could bull my way out our kitchen door and into freedom's compelling call, my mother said, "Not so fast. I want to hear exactly where you're off to and when you promise to be home."

"I gotta work on an English project. It's for school, Mom. Honest it is."

My mother, with hands on her hips, turned around from the stove to face me, raising an eyebrow. "What kind of project?"

"Miss Crowder assigned us to select a famous charac-

ter and then write up a whole page report about who-
ever we pick. We're working in teams of two for research. But we each have to write on it."

"Who's on *your* team?"

"Just two people. Me and another kid."

In the nick of time I held back spilling that my teammate was Banjo. That would have been super stupid.
Ferguson Hale Byler was not any mother's dream of a
suitable companion for her darling little angel boy. So,
I figured the less I said about Banjo, the safer I'd stay.
Besides, he lived close to the spar mine, a place where I
had been warned not to trespass.

"I best hurry or I'll be late."

"Where are you going?"

I lied. "To the Freemont Library and maybe to some
other places to dig up a famous character."

"Just be home by supper, Alvin." With a barrel of
oatmeal in me, I don't guess Mom reckoned that I'd be
needing any lunch.

"Okay. So long, Mom."

The Bylers lived about half a mile away, up Hanson
Road, beyond where the blacktop surface dead-ended
and became not much fancier than two wagon ruts.
Mrs. Byler roosted eleven children. There wasn't any
Mr. Byler; and, to my memory, there never had been
one. Among the eleven kids, Banjo nestled along in the
middle. He was number six. How his ma ever mustered

up the courage to produce more, after eying him, was no easy guess.

Not once had I ever spotted Banjo with his shirt tucked in. He was one original mess. A real curiosity. At a fair, people might even buy tickets to see him in a cage. He never looked washed or ironed. His hair was a gritty mat of disorder that would have discouraged a mule brush.

Yet I liked him. How could you hate a kid who had a grin that cracked open fresher than a raw egg?

The Byler house was a beat-up tarpaper shack with no glass in the windows. Just plastic. I'd been there before. Lots of times. Their shack was small, even smaller with eleven kids swarming. Like always, it was surrounded by at least a dozen scrawny chickens. Nearing the house, I yelled.

"You home, Banjo?"

The door squeaked open and out he popped. No shoes, no socks; just wearing his usual raggy clothes and dirty feet. Plus his trademark, his banjo, slung across his back on a length of clothesline that wouldn't have held up a damp bandana.

"Alvin! How ya be?"

It was like Banjo hadn't seen me in a hundred years instead of only yesterday. He sure had spirit. As I got closer I smelled Banjo, and he sure was alive. It was easy to tell whenever he got within nostril range.

"Okay," I said. "Where'll we go to nail down our famous character for Monday?"

Banjo winked. "I thought us up a dilly." Tucked under his arm was a wrinkled-up sack of brown paper. But it bulged.

"What's in the bag?"

"Lunch," said Banjo. "I packed ample for the both of us. Let's leg it."

We nosed ourselves uproad, not at all in the direction of the town of Freemont or its public library. The thought pricked me a mite.

"Where we headed?" I asked.

"It's a secret place, Alvin. Don't nobody know about this particular spot except for me. And maybe just one other person who happens to be our famous character, the one I aim for us to study and write about."

Picking a long-stem daisy, Banjo threaded it carefully through one of the forty-three holes in his shirt. The flower seemed content to ride along, as if it had been waiting by the roadside in order to smile up at him.

"Yup," said Banjo, "you and Miss Crowder are going to be right proud of me for thinking this one up. Won't nobody in the whole schoolhouse match *our* famous character."

"I give up," I told Banjo Byler. "Who is it?"

He grinned at me. "Jake Horse."

## · Five ·

I stopped dead. "You're kidding."

"Nope," said Banjo. "Miss Crowder told us to be inventive and select a very famous person, didn't she?"

I nodded, feeling a hint of breakfast oatmeal steal up into my throat. And also thinking about last night when I'd used a certain Jake Horse to spook Marybell, as well as myself, out of a peaceful sleep. It sort of bothered me some.

"Yessiree," Banjo went on to say, "most every tongue in Freemont wags about old Jake Horse. So, the way I cipher it all up, he's gotta be more than famous enough to pencil down."

Banjo was right.

On plenty of evenings, when Mom and Dad assumed that both Bell and I were asleep, I'd gone on tiptoe out to the top of the stairs to hear them whisper about Jake the hermit. And his mule. Plus how he lived all to his lonesome and never ventured down into Freemont, not even on a Saturday night.

My father had told Mom that he'd heard that Jake Horse was the only man in the entire county who still used a muzzle-load rifle. Jake's old gun, Dad said, was at least six foot long. Maybe even seven. And at a distance of better than a hundred yards, he could cut the hum off a hummingbird.

According to what my father whispered to my mother, I was recalling, Jake Horse just plain hated people. He hadn't always. But he grew right bitter when the mine got closed. The company ordered the miners to pack up and cart their families away from the mountain. So they all up and took leave.

All, that is, except Jake Horse.

Some folks kind of figured that Jake was dead. Because nobody ever saw him. It was only his ghost, Dad said, that played a ghostly white banjo from deep inside the maw of the mine. And the music crept out into the night's darksome like a wolf's howl, warning all us still-alive folks to keep distant and never to pesky around where he lived with his old mule.

My mother said that Alice Trowbridge, that's Ida's mother, told her that Jake Horse's mule was whiter than snow. Dead white, like the sheet of a midnight ghost on Halloween.

"What's wrong, Alvin?"

"Huh?" I suddenly looked at Banjo.

"Gee," he said, "you're standing stiller than a stone statue in the middle of the road, shaking all over. Maybe you took yourself a fever."

"Naw," I told him, rubbing the goose bumps off one arm and then the other, "I'm okay. Fitter than fettle. I was just thinking about maybe we could skip into town, visit the library, and do our report on George Washington."

"You serious?"

"Well," I said, "the town librarian, Mrs. Sample, sure is a friendly soul. Big around, too. Nobody'd ever claim Mrs. Sample was a ghost."

"You think Jake Horse is a ghost, Alvin?"

The way Banjo asked his question started my neck to itch, so scratchy that I was tempted to turn tail for home and oatmeal. "Nope," I said, "I don't guess he is."

"Me neither. Besides, the story goes that old Jake

plays a banjo good as me. Anybody who picks a banjo can't be all sour. So let's move."

As we walked up the road, kicking pebbles, the morning really bloomed. Sunlight sifted down through the high pines to play tag with the red squirrels and a twitter of sparrows. There was a shy wind, but it had come up here only to learn how to whisper. High above a patch of green and yellow willows, a flying crow drew quiet black circles on a blue sky.

Yet I wasn't thinking too much about the crow. Instead, I was recalling a warning that my mother issued, usually about twenty times a week: "Alvin Dickinson, you keep yourself clear of that awful old spar mine. Hear?"

"Yes'm," I always said.

Yet here we were, Banjo and I, trudging uproad toward the spar mine. Maybe, I thought, remembering what Miss Crowder had said only yesterday, writing a report about Robert E. Lee, or some other general, wasn't so dumb an idea.

Trailing up the wagon road, higher and higher, we let it lead us smack to the big structures at the mouth of the old spar mine.

One giant silo after another, eight in all, leaned against its brothers. Each silo looked about fifty feet high. Above the row of silos, a diagonal conveyor shoot connected their tops. Here the mountain slanted sharply upward so that each silo sprouted up higher than its downhill neighbor. Above the uppermost silo was a huge crusher box. Bigger than most of the houses in Freemont. Except maybe Mayor Swickert's.

At a respectful distance, the outbuildings of the spar mine didn't look so big. Yet the closer we walked, the more awesome it grew. Eight round giants, angry and ready for war. As a board creaked, I darn near turned and ran; instead, I held my ground. Once, a year or so ago, we'd gone on a Sunday school hike and had seen the spar mine from a mile or so away. Up close, it was one chilling sight.

I felt cold.

Quiet, I was thinking, sure can be more spooky than noise. And the eight gray silo giants were quieter than death.

"Banjo," I said in a very low voice, "I don't guess I like it here."

"You don't?"

"Leastwise, not a whole lot."

"How come you don't like the spar mine, Alvin? After all, it ain't ever done nothin' to you."

"No," I said to Banjo, "and I don't aim to hang around until it does."

Banjo Byler shifted his brown bag to under his op-

posite arm. "What's wrong? You're looking a mite on the pallid side."

I couldn't stop shaking. Or squinting up at the eight giant silos that stood together tighter than the fingers of a fist. All I could think was just one very uncomfortable thought:

Jake Horse was maybe the ghost of a dead mountain king, and this giant spar mine had once been his castle.

# · Six ·

"Come on, Alvin."

"Where to?" I asked Banjo.

"I'll show ya a hunk of real sport. First we climb to where the crusher box is. There's a ladder up it."

I pointed. "Way up *there?*"

Banjo smiled. "Let's be off."

He was right so far. We did find an old wooden ladder—and near to every other rung was busted. Or halfway cracked. Banjo's dirty feet led the way. As I followed, below him, I was praying that the ancient ladder would be sturdy enough to support his weight plus my own.

Banjo Byler claimed he weighed near to a hundred pounds, a lot of which had to be dirt. All I weighed was seventy-nine pounds, and that included half a ton of my mother's oatmeal.

The ladder shook. Feeling it, I closed my eyes and froze to the rotted rails.

"Keep climbing," yelled Banjo from above me. "We're darn near up to home free. *Yahoo!*"

Somehow, we both made it all the way to the top. Up here it felt much more windy. Even a bit cold. All the wood of the struts that framed the mighty crusher box looked gray and tired. It made me wonder how long ago the spar mine was active. People in Freemont always said that the lode had played itself out, so the miners stacked up their wagons and pulled stakes, leaving the old mine to its lonesome.

All, that is, except Jake Horse.

Banjo wiggled his bare toes. "Ain't it simple great up here, Alvin? Ain't it grand?"

Both my hands clung to a rusted axle on one of the big gear wheels. "Yeah," I told him, worrying if the old ladder would be good for one more pair of trips. "How come we had to monkey way up here?"

"To put down our lunch." Banjo pointed out over the trees. "And to see. From up here on top of the crusher, we can scan for miles in all directions. Hey, we might even be able to squint old Jake Horse before he spots us. Or hear his banjo."

"You ever seen him?" I asked Banjo.

"Nope. But maybe right now he's watching *us*."

I didn't cotton to the notion that maybe, right now, we were perhaps being watched by an old pair of eyes. It made me so nervous that I could hardly choke down lunch.

"Some say Jake's half Mohawk Indian," said Banjo, "and the other half is just mountain man."

"Well, even if he's half mountain *goat*," I said, "I sure don't see anybody up here. Except a crazy kid with a banjo on his back. Let's skin back down that ladder while it's still standing."

I felt the rust scratching rough on the palms of both hands. The iron was cold and lonely. Sort of deadly, as if no other hand but mine had touched it in a long spell.

"Here's what's fun," said Banjo.

The two of us were sitting on a square of gray beams that formed the very peak of the frame that capped off the feeder cone of the crusher box. The big box was shaped like an upside-down pyramid that wore an upside-down dishpan for a cap. And we were up on top of it all. I felt like a speck in the sky.

"What's fun?" I asked Banjo.

"Watch this."

Getting up from where he had straddled one of the gray beams, he crept over to the place where a trough fed out from the crusher bin.

"What are you planning to do?"

"We can work our way from the first silo down to the top of the lowest one. Come on, Alvin. It'll be real sport."

My hands tightened on the iron. "Are you out of your skull?"

"Nope. I done it once. It's a lead-pipe cinch. So come on and get yourself cranked."

Because I didn't want Ferguson Byler to squeal to all the guys at school about what a chicken I was, I followed him. We sure were up in the altitude. The trough was V-shaped, slanting downward. Apart a yard, metal paddles dotted the spine chain that belted through the trough; paddles that had once, I imagined, hauled the ore down to be fed into one silo or another.

Beneath my foot, the old chain nudged.

It made me sweat all over. In one second, writing about Stonewall Jackson did not seem to be such a dumb idea. At least he never lived atop a spar mine.

As my grip cautiously slid along the lip of the trough, I got pricked by a splinter. Breaking off, it buried in the heel of my hand.

I stopped.

"Hurry up, Alvin."

To hurry was exactly what I was *not* about to do. Mom's warning about the spar mine and its dangers crept into my brain. Especially about the cave-in, years back; three miners had been killed. And later on, Rote Colton had climbed up the outside of one of the silos, slipped, and been found dead.

"Hey! Are you coming or not?"

Banjo was twenty feet below me, on a slant, working his way over the uppermost silo. The bottoms of his feet were red from chain rust. He didn't seem to care. His old faded blue shirt was flapping loose beneath his banjo.

Gritting my teeth, I crept along after him, praying I wouldn't trip a misstep and tumble over the edge. Just below me was the tip of a pine tree, close enough to count the buds of its tiny cones, looking like a herd of tan mice. Beyond, over the green treetops, I saw the spires of Freemont, plus the gold dome of our town library. Wow, if Mrs. Sample could see me now, I'd wave.

"Wait up, Banjo."

"Okay, but let's go. We still got a hermit to corner and our reports to write."

"Well," I said, creeping an inch lower, "we haven't done either one, so I don't guess our fingers are going to cramp too much from writing. We'll never corner *any-body* up here in the yonder."

"Oh, he's up here on the mountain somewhere," Banjo insisted, "still lingering."

"Then how do we smoke him out?"

Banjo Byler scratched his rump. "I don't guess I rightly know, Alvin. I'll have to ponder it a spell."

"Ponder all you like. I'm going back up to the crusher box and climb down the ladder. One slip, and we could—" I couldn't finish my thoughts. It was too hair-raising. This old spar mine was grayer and deader than a winter chill. A sad place. Above me, the black mouth of the mine tunnel seemed to yawn out a silent scream.

I heard a sharp crack. Twisting my head around to look downward, I couldn't see Banjo. He was gone.

He'd fallen.

# · Seven ·

"Banjo!"

The echo of my yell took several long seconds to die. My mouth fell open and felt bone dry, like I wasn't hog-calling to anyone except ghosts. I roared out his name again. "Banjo!"

"Alvin. . . ."

His voice hit my ear, coming from a far piece away. But where?

Creeping along the old shoot to the place where I had last seen him, I peered down into the dark and deep silo bin. And I could see Banjo kicking in the air like some sort of weird buzzard, flapping his arms. What I saw clearest was a white spot, round as a supper plate, the pan of his banjo that was still roped to his back, as it usually was.

"Banjo?"

"Help me. Quick!" His answer floated up to me from the half darkness of the silo. Then, beside my own foot, I discovered the busted strut of rotten gray wood that must have given way before he tumbled.

Banjo was suspended in space, about twenty-five feet below me, by what looked like the tail of his shirt snagged on one of the feeder hooks. Had the arm of that agitator not been where it was, all those years, the pit of the silo would have claimed a boy's broken body.

"Alvin . . . I'm choking. Help me."

"Hold on. I'll turn you free."

An iron bar grew up through the center of the empty silo. Every few feet, gear cleats encircled the bar, small discs of iron hardly bigger than doughnuts. Leaning out, I couldn't quite reach the bar. Clinging to one of the chain links with my left hand, I stretched over the silo's yawning pit until the tip of my middle finger rubbed the iron bar. It felt gritty. Yet that was as far as I dared reach.

There was only one way. To let go and jump, hoping I could catch the vertical bar that wore the string of doughnuts and hang tight, then work my way down.

"Hurry—hurry. . . ." Banjo's voice sounded peppered with pain.

I leaped out over the black nothing below me, watching my fingers grab the iron, then feeling my body meet it too. The bar kicked hard between my legs, as if it knew where to kick a boy to hurt the worst. I near folded up sick. Yet I couldn't double up my body, even though I felt both my knees jack.

"Alvin?"

"Yeah," I grunted. "Hang on tough."

The toe of my right sneaker felt one of the iron doughnuts, and I offered it some weight, slipping my hands as my fingers felt the hard iron snake upward through my fists. As the first uprushing doughnut hit my hands, it tore the bar from my grip. Fighting to regrab it, my lip smashed against the steel. One more doughnut floated up, passing my face; then another, and a third. Falling, I lost count. Only by locking both legs around the bar did I stop myself.

"Alvin. . . ."

Twisting around, I slipped down the bar for one more doughnut, reaching Banjo. His shirt was snagged on some outcrop of metal, sort of like a blunt hook. Cloth pulled tightly around his throat, choking him. That, plus his banjo rope. Both his hands and bare feet swam in empty air.

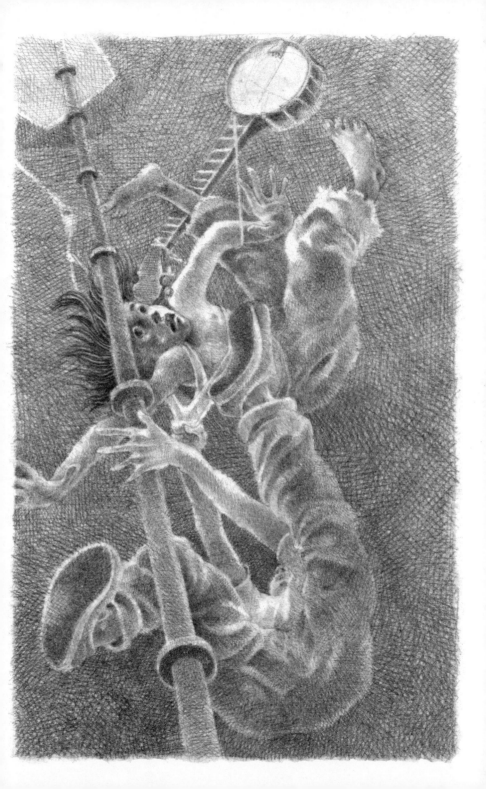

Somehow I stabbed my left hand upward, through his belt, fighting off his fingers as they clawed at my face. It was like Banjo was drowning in the shadowy space. Holding the bar as firmly as possible, I muscled one mighty yank, and heard his shirt rip. His body leaped at me, both arms and both legs grabbing at me, the bar, and the empty nothing all around us.

We were sure to fall.

No longer could I hold on. One rising doughnut exploded into the underside of my hands, breaking my grip. Two long seconds later we hit the crushed stone below. I should have closed my eyes. Too late. Sharp fragments of what must have been ore shattered in my eyes on the impact.

Then nothing.

Only blackness and fearful pain, feeling hard hunks of stone cutting my face. My eyes were clenched shut, hurting. Was I blind? My eyes sure were smarting. One opened to see nothing, and prickles forced me to close it again.

"Banjo?"

No answer.

"Hey! Where are ya, Banjo?"

"Alvin. . . ."

Lifting an arm, I moved it forward, feeling nothing except chunks of rock. I nudged my other shoulder. All my bones hurt. Yet my arms weren't busted. I tried one leg. Okay; then the other. Reaching out again, my fingers were rewarded with a face.

"Banjo?"

"I'm dead."

"No you're not. But I bet you hurt all over like me."

My fingers felt his head nod. "Are you really okay, Alvin?"

"I'm okay except for my eyes. They sorry the worst because it hurts too sassy to open 'em up."

Banjo didn't say anything. But I could sense, in the dark, that there was something he wasn't telling me.

"I'm glad you're okay," he said.

"Come on, Banjo. Tell me what's wrong."

"Nothing."

"You're a liar, Banjo Byler, so let's have it straight out."

I felt him flinch, and then he told me what was wrong. He sure let me have it full forward.

"Alvin, my leg's broke."

# · Eight ·

I quit breathing. "You sure?"

"Wow, am I sure. When I move, my old leg just flops. It's clean busted."

"Does it hurt a whole lot?"

Banjo tried to fake a laugh. He didn't sound too happy. "No, not a heavy lot. It's strange, but I don't hardly feel nothing in it at all. Like my leg's fixing to go to sleep. See? It flops limp."

My eyes wouldn't open. It felt like somebody had

removed both my eyeballs and replaced them with cin-
ders. Or broken glass.

"I'm blind, Banjo. Or near to."

"No," he said. "It's just so dreadful dark down here
wherever we be."

"Can you see anything?" I asked him. "How are you
lying?"

"I'm on my back, sort of. All I see's a round spot of
blue, way up yonder. Just a circle of sky."

"How far up?"

Banjo sighed. "A long ways. Looks like that there
circle of sky is located about a inch this side of
Heaven."

I rolled closer to him so we'd be nearby for each
other. All I wanted to do was touch him some so's I
wouldn't feel so alone.

"Here," said Banjo, "feel my leg. *You* might as well,
because I sure as hankering can't feel it."

Banjo's leg felt loose and cold. Even though the rest
of him was warm. Funny, but I didn't mind his smell. It
was barely bothersome.

"How are your eyes? Any better?"

I tried to open each eye but then quit trying. "Not
much." They both still hurt plenty.

"Somebody'll find us, Alvin." As he spoke, Banjo
Byler didn't sound too convincing.

Lying beside him, I recalled lying to Mom, telling her I'd be at the Freemont Library. Tonight, when it came suppertime, she'd telephone the library. And then Mrs. Sample would tell my mother that she hadn't seen me in days. I'd die a liar. Right then, I even missed Marybell.

"I wish my mother was here," I told Banjo. "Right now." As I said it, my voice was sort of shaking; yet I didn't give a hoot. Being blind and dying sure wasn't a whole lot of fun, even on Saturday, so all I could think to do next was cry. I just lay there sobbing, my head on Banjo Byler's chest.

He rested one arm around my shaking shoulders and said, "Hey, it's okay, Alvin. It'll be okay. I'm afraid, too. I swear, if'n I ever git out of this here fix we're in, I might even up and wash."

I couldn't answer. So I just sobbed. Even when I tried to talk, the words were all so wobbled that not one sounded like a wisp of sense. Not even to me. We didn't speak for a while. I don't guess I knew for how long. Then I began to be aware that my eyes hurt less. Perhaps all my bawling flushed out some of the little hunks of grit. Trying hard, I could finally open my left eye a slit; yet there sure was precious little to see. Except gloom. Plus an out-of-reach blue spot of sky.

"Smile," said Banjo. He presented my ribs with a good solid nudge.

"There's nothing to smile over."

"Yes, there is, sport. We're alive. And we're going to live to get ourselfs up and clear free. Hear?"

I nodded. "How?"

"*That*," he said, "is only our next problem. What pleases me is that we still got the guts to tackle what needs to be done."

"Darn you, Banjo. You and your bright ideas got us into this mess, so start getting us out. I want to go home. And the report I'll write is about this damn fool I got for a pal. *You*. And I don't care whether Miss Crowder gives me a *A* or a *F*."

Banjo chuckled. "If'n you write about *me*, Alvin, you'll get a *A* automatic."

"I wish Miss Crowder was here."

Banjo looked at me in the gloom. "How come?"

"Because I like her, that's why. She's a good teacher and she tries righteous hard. When she doesn't know something, she always blurts out to admit it."

"I like her too."

This surprised me. "You do?"

"Honest," said Banjo. "Even when she chews me out, because it's her job to work us onto the straight and narrow. Do you know why I blow spit bubbles during spelling?"

"No, tell me."

"Because," said Banjo, "I want Miss Crowder to notice me. I like it when she says my name—*Ferguson Byler*—like I'm really somebody."

"That's because she likes you, Banjo."

"Nobody likes *me*. Except you. You're my only friend, Alvin." He tried to sit up. "That's why I got to git you out of here. The only things that matter to me, outside of Ma and my family, is you and my banjo."

I felt his body twitch. "You okay?" I asked.

"Hey!" he said. "Where is it, Alvin? Where's my banjo?" His voice was pure panic.

I didn't want Banjo to cry. Nor did I want him to find his banjo all broken. That would be too tough for him to take.

"Easy," I said. "I'll find it. Lie back."

But he wouldn't. As I groped along the ore in the dark I could hear him crawling, searching, actually panting to find his precious banjo. For him, losing it would be near as sad as losing his life.

My hand touched something. "Here it is."

"Is it busted? Fetch it over to me, Alvin. I gotta know. I just gotta hold it to me and hug it tender."

Dragging the banjo over to where he lay, I handed it to him, feeling his hands tremble as he took it.

"Merciful Moses," said Banjo. "It ain't busted."

## · Nine ·

*Thwank!*

Banjo strummed a chord. He was lying in the dark, plunking it, and humming out happy. *Plankety-plank-plank.* And he sure could make it talk. Yet it didn't sound as full as usual.

"You sure it isn't busted, Banjo?"

"Nope. But one of her strings got snapped. Other than that, she's prime. Hot diggity doghouse! She's all to one piece."

He *is* crazy, I thought. Ferguson Hale Byler is bananas. The fall knocked his brains out of whack. Yet he'd always been nuts. But, I remembered, he'd also always been wonderful. Anytime a kid at school got to crying, Banjo would always trot over, tune up, and sing the kid a song to dry up the tears.

Miss Crowder saw him do it. More than once. Maybe this was why she let him get away with so much mischief, because knowing Banjo Byler was just so downright worthwhile.

Now he was actually singing and playing "You Are My Sunshine." I couldn't believe it. Even on three strings instead of four, his chords rang near to okay in *my* ear.

"*You make me happy*," sang Banjo, "*when skies are gray.*"

There he is, I thought, playing and singing to his broken leg. At school, he couldn't spell cat or catch a baseball. But he was one great kid.

He stopped singing. "Alvin, I got it!"

"Got what? Some new brand of disease?"

"No, I honest got us a way out."

"How?"

"We'll *sing* our way home."

I fought the urge to cry again. It isn't easy suddenly to realize that a pal has ruptured his reason. Banjo had. He now had spit where his brains should have been.

"Byler," I said, "this is it. You finally did it. I hereby

declare you a genuine boob. Congratulations. You're now officially nuts. If I had time, I'd get you a certificate."

"No, I'm not crazy. Never was and never will be. All we do, Alvin, is just sing until someone *hears* us. If we shout, that's only two of us. But if we *sing*, it'll be you and me and my banjo."

So we sang.

We belted out "Turkey in the Straw."

But it was more yelling than singing. Inside the belly of that big silo our noise surely did bounce around. What an echo. We must have sounded a note or two shy of the United States Marine Band. Next we polished off "The Moon Shines Tonight on Pretty Red Wing," and "Zip Coon." But then, when we attempted "Oh Bury Me Not on the Lone Prairie," our tonsils just weren't into it. In fact, the *bury me not* part made us both pull up short.

The silence was black and cold; even harder than our rocky bed of ore.

I heard it! A sudden noise that reached us from a long way off. I felt my friend stiffen because he had heard it too.

A banjo.

Maybe, I thought, I'm now as crazy as this Byler kid. I lay there wondering if insanity was really contagious. Yet the sound kept coming. Sometimes it would melt away, very faintly, then die. But after a minute or two would pass, back it came. Yet never closer. Was it testing us? Again I heard the ghostly banjo fade away into stillness. Maybe, I told myself, it was only our echo.

Neither one of us said anything. We only listened.

I heard it again. Sure enough, it was a banjo playing. And it wasn't Banjo Byler's. Whatever it was, it was flirting with us, teasing us, trying to get us to lose our senses. I could have sworn that I heard the familiar chords of "Pretty Red Wing."

Banjo moved, making ready his hands. This time when the ghost banjo quit, my friend took over, continuing the music where the distant notes cut off. It was so cussed spooky that I thought my spine had froze up.

Silence again.

Banjo waited it out. One minute—two—five—near to ten. But when the banjo finally poked through the quiet, I knew it was closer by a mile. I even recognized the tune, which would have pleased my mother. She was always urging Marybell or me to cultivate a deeper ear for music. Mom, I thought, you should witness me now.

The tune I recognized was "Wabash Cannonball."

Banjo hit on it first. Way early. There wasn't a song written, sung, or danced to that Banjo Byler couldn't handle.

Then it stopped.

I waited, hearing nothing—nothing at all. It was over. All I could think about was the fact that we'd never get out. We'd both perish. I'd never get to complete my birdhouse for Mother's Day. It was too sorrowful to bear, because soon Mom wouldn't have a birdhouse or a son.

"Mom!" I yelled. I couldn't help it.

"Hush," said Banjo. "Listen up."

I sweated all over. "What is it?"

"Footsteps. Somebody's coming, Alvin."

"I can't hear anything."

"Not if you keep on talking thataway. Try to hush your mug and listen."

I heard it too, from way above us. The chain rattled in the shoot. It made me hitch over an inch closer to Banjo. Then, looking straight up at our high circle of sky, I saw something crack the edge of the perfect circle.

It was a black hat.

# · Ten ·

"Ho!"

When I heard the voice, my entire body sweated up in less than a breath, all over. The voice was dry, brittle, the way you'd expect a ghost to whisper. More of a hiss than a holler.

"Banjo," I whispered, my mouth up real close to my pal's ear, "do you reckon he can vision us down here?"

Banjo didn't answer. Maybe, like me, he was too scared to speak up. Yet he did something else. When he did it, I thought the fright would near to kill me on the spot. His hand hit the strings of his banjo to whang out a three-note chord.

Above us, the hat moved. "You busted something."

How, I wondered, did the stranger know about Banjo's broken leg? Only a ghost could see in the dark, down this deep, and know about our secrets and our trouble.

"Yup," the dry old voice cackled again, "I oughta let you tarry there and rot. So's you don't nose around here no more."

Banjo hit his chord again. *Plink.*

"Ya don't fool me none." The old voice sounded hoarse. Dryer than a scratch. "You must a' busted her up proper."

"Sure did," said Banjo. "It's my E string that got clean busted."

That dumb and crazy pal of mine never even mentioned his leg bone. All he fretted about was his stupid old banjo.

"You play rightly fine," the voice said down to us. "Better on three strings than me on four. But you don't belong here. Nobody do. Best I learn ya not to pester folks."

I felt Banjo stiffen up. "Please—"

"You alone down there, banjo boy?"

"No," I said, slightly astounded at my own courage to speak up and get counted. "I'm down here too. My name's Alvin Dickinson and I want to go home."

The man's head and hat jerked away, and the circle of blue above our heads looked whole again.

"He's gone," I told Banjo. "We spooked him clean away. There's a hateful in his voice that I don't trust."

"Maybe he'll fetch back with help."

"You think so?"

"I honest do, Alvin. Because it sure won't ease our minds much to reason otherwise."

Well, I thought, that makes sense. Ferguson Byler had himself a knack for viewing matters on the bright side.

As it turned out, Banjo was right. The old hat peeked down at us again, asking, "You two still put?"

"Yessir," said Banjo, "we're real put."

"Honest," I said. "You won't find anybody around these parts more *put* than Banjo and me."

"I brung a rope," the voice said. "Even though you don't deserve it."

Sure enough, despite the old man's cussing, I spotted one end of a rope snaking down our way. As its loops twisted and turned in the half light, it made me wonder who'd get to be the first one up. I was lighter than Banjo, a lot lighter, so I made the decision to go first.

"Loop it under your arms," the old voice yelled down to us.

"Best I go first, Banjo. I don't weigh as much as you

do. That way I can help haul you up when it comes your turn. Okay?"

Banjo nodded. "I know you won't leave me here alone," he said. "It just ain't your style."

My fist punched his shoulder. Not hard. "Count on it," I said.

The rope was rough and scratched like a sinner's soul on Sunday. Something fearful. Yet it was a good feeling. I threaded myself into it and started up.

"Pull," yelled Banjo. "And please don't drop him. He's my only friend. Besides, he might land on my banjo."

Going up wasn't near as quick as going down. It was slow work. Yet the spot above me was swelling up bigger and bigger, and I did my level best not to glance down at Banjo, far below. I just kept kicking and scratching my way up. It was odd because I still couldn't catch a glimpse of the person on the other end of the rope. Somebody was pulling, that was for doggone sure. I was getting hauled up, up, up.

I made it to the top, hooked a leg over into freedom, and was met by a tough old face. Real olden. A face that looked empty and spent.

But he had eyes that looked right through me as if they knew what a silly kid I was to get trapped in the pit of a spar mine silo. His jaw sported a gray beard, and he didn't seem to have any teeth. Pulling a red

bandana from out of a back pocket, the old man dusted the ore dust from my face very gently.

Then he loosened the slipknot on the rope so that I could turn loose. His hand clapped me on the shoulder, and he shook his head like he couldn't believe he hauled me up to liberty.

"Thanks a whole lot, mister," I said. "My name is Alvin Dickinson, but I guess I already told you."

"Howdy," he said. "I'm Jake Horse."

# · Eleven ·

I couldn't breathe.

All I could do was sit there on the ramp with my back leaning against the rim of the silo, staring at the old gentleman who had just now admitted his identity.

"Jake . . . Horse?"

He nodded a sour look at me. "I know, boy. You thunk I was dead." He tossed his rope into the silo pit and let it out real easy, hand over hand. "I ain't."

"Thanks a lot, Mr. Horse."

"Forgit it. We got another soul down yonder to fetch

up. You the kid who picks a banjo?" He pointed at his own instrument, which was lying on the gray boards.

"No," I confessed. "Not me."

Mr. Horse snuffed his nose. "Figured as much. Had that banjo below been yourn, I don't guess you'd a' come up without it."

Thinking about my pal, I smiled, shaking my head. "You're right about that."

"Figured. I could reason by how he played it that he cared for the doggone thing, same as I cotton to mine. Since my mule, Essie, died off, it be about all I do care for. I don't cotton to people. But a banjo's fair company."

Looking at Mr. Horse, I should have been scared skinny. But I wasn't. His rough voice had softened as he'd mentioned his banjo. I was sorry his mule died. Yet glad he had a banjo to love.

"Hey!"

Peeking over the rim's edge and down into the silo pit, I yelled down to Banjo Byler, who, I could tell by his holler, was getting a mite itchy to climb up and join us. I felt a bit worried if the sour old man would do a second hauling.

"Mr. Horse, we'll have to take it easy hauling up my friend. His leg's broken."

"Honest?"

I nodded.

We pulled together, and it sure was tough work, seeing as how Banjo packed more beef on his bones than I did. For the last twenty feet, I figured my hands were fixing to burn up the rope; yet I didn't quit. Mr. Jake Horse looked sturdy built. He was one of those old-timers who had been cut out of barbed wire; skinny and tripe tough.

We fished Banjo up, along with his instrument. His face was pale and wet with the worry that we might let loose of the rope to let him fall. His leg flopped useless, and I saw his face sour with pain.

"Yup," said Mr. Horse, easing my friend down to comfortable, "you sure do got a busted wheel." Even if his voice was tough, the old man's hands appeared to be gentle as he touched Banjo's leg.

"I honest do," said Banjo.

The two of us, the old gentleman and me, dragged Banjo back along the shoot chain, and again using the rope, lowered him down along the busted ladder, near the crusher. We climbed down the rickety ladder, the old man with his banjo and me with a prayer.

"Hold it," said Mr. Horse.

As he cussed, I watched him tear a loose board off a shed door and then ribbon a splint around Banjo's bad leg. It looked neater than a Christmas present. When he was through his doctoring, he looked at me, and then back to Banjo.

"Thanks," he grunted.

"It ought to be us thanking you, Mr. Horse," I told him. "You saved us."

"Wrong." His mouth bent a grin. "I been alone too long."

Mr. Horse fished a knife from his pocket to cut a pair of poles. He and I used our shirts to dress it into a stretcher to tote Banjo home.

Getting to Banjo's took a tough hour.

I intended to introduce Mrs. Byler to Mr. Horse; yet never got the chance, because the old gentleman sort of melted off into the trees and was gone. Vanished without a word. It made me feel kind of sorry that I really didn't quite thank him proper.

"Alvin," said Mrs. Byler, "maybe you best hike to Freemont and fetch back Doc Butler. He's the only doctor who'll come away out here. Tell him I ain't got the cash to pay his bill, but if'n he'll take a chicken sometime, I'll make it square."

"Right," I said.

I ran every step into town, found Doc Butler, and asked him to visit the Bylers. He never dickered about the chicken. All he did was hustle me into his Plymouth, and we really kicked dust. But then he stopped the car and told me I wouldn't be needed and to go right straight home. And pronto.

"But I want to help you frost on a cast," I told him. "I can be a real big help."

"Go home and wash," he told me. "Because if you don't, your folks might not know who you are and throw you back in the coal pile. If you were to crawl out from under my sink, I'd spray you with Flit. How in Hades did you get that dirty?"

"At the spar mine," I told Doc as I climbed out of his Plymouth. "Ferguson Byler and I found Jake Horse and fell into a silo, all the way to the bottom."

Doc's eyebrows raised. "For real?"

"Yes. That's how Ferguson broke his leg and we hauled him up on a rope."

"Out of a spar silo?"

I nodded.

"Kids." Doc snorted, gunning his gas pedal. "You all ought to get cooped in a pit until you're twenty-one. Freemont don't need a school. We need a stockade."

He drove off.

# · Twelve ·

Marybell caught me.

It was dark, and I was trying to sneak into the house through the back door, but there she was. The look on my sister's face told me that she didn't recognize me at first. But it didn't take her long to crack a secret.

"Alvin's home!"

"Hush," I warned her. Too late. Looking up from where I sat on the back porch, emptying ore dust out of one sneaker, I saw Mom. And she sure saw me.

"You're really going to get it now," I heard Bell

whisper with her nail-bitten hand covering half of her impish grin. It made me realize that maybe I'd bullied her some and perhaps I'd best quit.

"Alvin Dickinson!" said my mother, as if it was her constant job to announce to the world who I was.

"Boy," I said to Mom, "are you lucky."

As I dumped dust from the other sneaker, my mother's eyes were swelling wider and wider as if she were trying to see all my dirt, cuts, and scratches with just one look.

"Where," she asked, "on Earth have you—"

What I liked the best about Mom was the fact that I always knew exactly what she was going to say. It was part of being home. Again, she came in right on cue.

"Just look at your clothes."

"I'm being considerate, Mom. See? I'm not tracking any of my dirt into your nice clean house."

"You missed supper," said Marybell, who was always a big help in matters of my self-defense.

As I saw my mother reach for the kitchen yardstick, I realized how fast I would have to talk. The only way to fight Mom's anger was with her own curiosity. I'd use the one word that would do it. "I've been in an *accident*."

Raised, her yardstick stopped in midair. But my safety was short-lived when Bell giggled. I wanted to murder all her dolls.

"Marybell," ordered Mom, "please go inside this very instant. Do you hear?"

"No, I want to watch you lick Alvin."

This last remark from my sister didn't do a lot to improve my mother's disposition. Yet it did help the confusion angle. Her yardstick couldn't seem to decide where to land first.

"Please don't be rude to Mom," I told Bell. "I think you ought to apologize and then maybe try to improve your manners."

My sister pointed at me. "He's trying to wiggle out of it."

Bell, I had to admit, was a lot like me. Genuine trouble. As my mother advanced a step in my direction, it was again time for an artful dodge.

"Mom," I asked, "have you ever seen a broken leg?"

Her mouth opened and remained refreshingly silent for at least two seconds. Yet it was too good to last. "Alvin, if this is one of your—"

Bell giggled.

"There's nothing funny about a broken bone," I told Marybell. "Doc Butler just brought me home. So if you don't believe it," I said, looking up at Mom, "just ask *him*."

My mother looked stunned. "Doctor Butler?"

"Yes'm," I said. "It's true. I may be dirty and badly hurt. But I'm not a liar."

"Yes he is," Bell mumbled. That sister of mine could really play cute. What annoyed me most is how well she knew my number.

It was difficult to determine which of the two was more confused, my mother or her yardstick. Neither one appeared to be totally convinced where punishment should begin or how many healthy whacks were needed to restore either order or cleanliness.

I was glad to see Dad open the kitchen door to join the party.

"All right," he said, pretending to take charge, even though every Dickinson in our family, including the cat, knew that Mom was the real boss, "what's the trouble? Alvin, where in Sam Hill have you—"

"Doctor Butler broke his leg," said Marybell.

Right then, I could have hugged her. Good old Bell really came through with one heck of a detour on the road to my getting whaled.

"Doc busted his leg?" As he asked the question, Dad looked at Mom. "Well, what are *you* planning to do, dear—go splint it with a yardstick?"

Mom looked as though she wanted to apply the yardstick to Dad, and *not* to his *leg*. It was a good time to recruit my father to my team, before he started commenting on how dirty I was.

"Dad," I said, "have I got news for you."

As next to nothing ever happened in Freemont, *news*,

to most local ears, was indeed a magic word. Magic because it always worked like a charm.

"News?" Dad's face brightened.

"No, it wasn't Doc Butler whose leg got busted. It was somebody else's."

Dad's eyebrows raised. "Whose?"

"Banjo's."

"You mean one of those crazy Byler kids who live in that old shack up on Hanson Road?"

I nodded. "Honest. He fell into a spar silo, and I had to help pull him out. And he's not really crazy. But you'll never guess who helped me rescue him, Dad."

Bell butted in. "Alvin's getting out of it again."

"What were you doing at the spar mine?" Mom wanted to know. As she asked the question, her yardstick lowered an inch or two, which usual flagged a good sign.

"Rescuing my friend." I grinned. "But I sure couldn't have hauled him up alone. Banjo Byler would still be down there, lying in pain on a pile of ore, if it hadn't been for Jake Horse."

Dad's glasses slid down his nose and he peered over the half-moon lenses. "No *kidding?*"

"Honest to Pete," I said.

Dad smiled, clapping me on the back. I could see how pleased he was as he turned to speak to Mom. "Irma, our boy's a hero." Dad beamed. "And if Alvin's a real hero, maybe he ought to get a medal or something."

"And not get licked," said Bell.

When she touched my hand, I knew my little sister was now on my side. It felt good to know.

"Bell," I told her, "you're okay."

# · Thirteen ·

The next morning, I really did pray.

As I sat in our pew, soaking in all my churching up, I thanked God for the first Sunday of my life that I was alive and whole, even saying a prayer for the old man who did for us. I was most grateful that we'd done for him too. It turned out to be a long Sunday. After church was over, I was not allowed out of the house because of yesterday's dirt. So I stayed in my room to write my report. For a bedtime story, I read it to Bell.

For some strange reason, next to my getting whaled,

nothing ever seemed to please Marybell more than to have me go to bed at the same time she went. So I did. My pillow felt really nifty, and so did welcoming the sunshine of a fresh Monday morning.

The biggest shock of all came when I got to school and saw Banjo already there, with a pair of homemade crutches tucked under his arms. And, of course, a banjo on his back.

"Alvin," he greeted me. "What's new?"

Actually, it was Ferguson Byler who looked new. Banjo was washed, his hair had been brushed, and he appeared cleaner than a caught fish. He wasn't wearing socks. But at least there wasn't a single speck of smudge on his one bare ankle. The white cast on his other leg looked the cleanest of all.

We all handed in our stories. Needless to say, Banjo and I were the only ones who had been smart enough to write about Freemont's most famous celebrity, Jake Horse.

"Well," said Miss Crowder, licking two gold stars with her tongue, one to slap on Banjo's report and the other on mine, "we may have at least two budding authors in our midst."

Turning around, Banjo winked my way.

I still couldn't quite recover from the jolt of seeing Banjo Byler so clean. Somehow, the ten new moons of black grit that usually ringed the edges of his fingernails had been plowed away. The only element of his personal appearance that remained the same was his smile. He still had a grin that would melt cheese.

Best of all, Miss Crowder took note of his change for the better. Our teacher was a believer in both soap and good manners, and it was now plain to see that Banjo Byler was no longer a foreigner to either one.

"I'm sorry about your leg, Ferguson," she told him. "But I'm so glad you didn't break your banjo." As she said it, she reached out and smoothed his hair. Then she let all of us sign our names, in red ink, on Banjo's white cast.

I was real glad it was Banjo's big day. And that the kids wanted to crowd in closer to Banjo than ever before. I guess Miss Crowder could see that Banjo was still hurting some, so she let him tell us all about our adventure up at the old spar mine and about how we finally got to meet Mr. Jake Horse. The kids really listened. Banjo, it turned out, was the best storyteller in the whole room.

"Yessir," said Banjo, pulling his banjo off his back, "there we were, just me an' Alvin here, alone in the darksome of a deserted silo pit."

Miss Crowder leaned an inch forward too, looking as anxious to hear the story as the rest of us. Even though I knew the entire yarn, I figured that Ferguson Byler would gussy it up all the way.

He did.

"And," Banjo finished, "that's how we called for help." He twanged a chord. "Then we heard an answering banjo, from afar off."

I liked what I saw. Ferguson Byler was being a hero for the first day in his life, instead of just that crazy kid who was always dirty and constantly laughed at. But when he described Mr. Horse as standing over ten foot tall, Miss Crowder suggested that perhaps my pal was getting a bit enthusiastic and an inch or so too elastic with the truth.

"Well," said Banjo, "up on top of a spar mine, men folks tend to look a mite taller than usual."

Miss Crowder smiled. "Yes, I imagine so." Then she looked right smack at me and said, "A boy can be tall too. Very tall."

Later on, when we were all supposed to be pouring over our geography books, and I was straining across the entire map of Asia in an effort to locate Peru, I sneaked a peek at my pal. He sat in front of me. So I could easily take careful notice of the banjo slung across his back.

It hit me!

I looked again. No, I wasn't dreaming. Because it's right simple to count up to four; and there they all were, right in front of my nose. There were now *four* strings on Banjo's banjo.

"Hey," I whispered, leaning forward to tap Banjo on the shoulder. "How come your banjo's back to normal?"

Banjo whispered back. "Alvin, you won't believe it even if'n I up and tell ya."

"Try me."

"It happened yesterday, Sunday morning. Right early, we heard a knock at the door, and you won't guess who it was."

"Who?" I asked.

"Mr. Jake Horse."

"Well, don't quit up. Finish the story."

Up front, Miss Crowder was busy, writing some unimportant stuff on the blackboard that had to do with homework. So I listened to my friend tell his tale.

"He come for breakfast, Alvin. And then, after we all did our food, Mr. Horse said it was Sunday morning, a special day, so he played us a hymn on his banjo."

"Then what?"

"He said that he wanted a present to bring me because of my busted leg, but he didn't have but one thing to give—something he hated to part with. So he unhooked the E string off his banjo and laced it to mine."

"Honest?"

Banjo nodded and cracked his best grin.

Well, I guess that's the story of why old Jake Horse's banjo no longer sounds the same up in the mountains. It's missing a string. Yet I figure we both gave him something to balance even. He said that Banjo and I had gifted him back his life.

I reckon Jake Horse reasoned that one worn E string was a fair price to pay.

ROBERT NEWTON PECK was born and raised in Vermont. He has been a farmer, a soldier, a lumberjack, a football player, and a hog butcher. But he says at heart he is still a Vermont farmer. He is also a prolific writer, an enthusiastic public speaker and in his spare time plays ragtime piano, tennis and the old Scottish game of curling. He is the author of *A Day No Pigs Would Die* and the popular *Soup* books, and won the 1982 Mark Twain Award for *Soup for President*. He lives with his wife and their two children in Longwood, Florida.